Kings and Queens

Philip Sauvain

WAYLAND

FAMOUS LIVES

Artists
Campaigners for Change
Engineers
Explorers
Inventors
Kings and Queens
Saints
Writers

Series Editor: Alex Woolf
Designer: Joyce Chester
Consultant: Norah Granger

First published in 1996 by Wayland Publishers Ltd,
61 Western Road, Hove, East Sussex, BN3 1JD

This edition published in 1998 by Wayland Publishers Ltd

© Copyright 1996 Wayland Publishers Limited

Find Wayland on the Internet at http://www.wayland.co.uk

British Library Cataloguing in Publication Data
Sauvain, Philip, 1933–
   Kings and queens. – (Famous lives)
   1.Kings and rulers – Juvenile literature
   2.Queens – Juvenile literature
   I.Title II.Series
   305.5'222

ISBN 0 7502 2296 4

Typeset by Joyce Chester
Printed by L.E.G.O. S.p.A., Vicenza, Italy

Picture acknowledgements
The publishers would like to thank the following for allowing
their pictures to be used in this book: Archiv für Kunst und
Geschichte/Erich Lessing 10 (top), 12, /Erich Lessing 15
(top), 15 (bottom); The Bridgeman Art Library,
London/Wallace Collection, London front cover (top left)
and 29, /Fishmongers' Hall, London front cover (bottom left)
and 29, /Musee de la Tapisserie, Bayeux (with special
authorisation of the city of Bayeux)/Giraudon 7, /Hever
Castle Ltd 10 (bottom), /Corsham Court, Wiltshire 16,
/Private Collection 19, /Private Collection 20 and 29, /King
Street Galleries, London 21, /Victoria & Albert Museum,
London 22; Camera Press 24, 25, 26, 27 (bottom); Mary
Evans Picture Library 13, 18 (bottom), 23 (bottom); Michael
Holford 4 and 28 (top), 5; Hulton Deutsch 17; Philip Sauvain
6, 9, 11, 14, 18 (top), 23 (top); Topham/Martin Keene 27
(top); Visual Arts Library front cover (right), 1, 8 and 28
(middle); Wayland Picture Library cover (background), 28
(bottom).

Contents

King William I

Over 900 years ago, the Saxon people lived in England. Their king was Edward. He and his wife had no children. After he died, a great lord called Harold became king. When William, Duke of the Normans, heard this he was angry. He was Edward's cousin. Edward had promised him that he would be the next king of England.

◁ William was the ruler of Normandy in France.

William decided to fight Harold for the throne. First of all he had to build ships to take his men across the sea. The Normans set sail from France. They landed near Hastings in Sussex and got ready to fight a great battle.

DATES	
1028	William I born
1066	William I becomes king
1087	Death of William I

△ Here are the Normans sailing to England.

During the battle William was knocked off his horse. Some Normans turned back, but he stopped them. *'Look at me well,'* he shouted. *'I am still alive. You are letting yourselves be killed. You are throwing away victory.'*

The Normans attacked the Saxons again. Many men died and King Harold was killed. William had won. He went on to conquer the rest of England. He became known as William the Conqueror.

A crown was put on William's head to show he was the king. This is called a coronation.

◁ This is what a coronation was like hundreds of years ago.

Some women made pictures to tell the story of how William became king. They sewed pieces of coloured wool on to a very long cloth. This is called a tapestry. You can see it today at Bayeux in France.

This picture from the Bayeux Tapestry shows a scene from the Battle of Hastings. ▽

In 1086, William decided to find out as much as he could about his new country. He sent men to find out how much land there was, and how many animals. They also found out how much each person owned. All this information was collected into a huge book called *Domesday Book*.

William died in 1087. All the kings and queens who ruled England later were related to him. No one else ever conquered England again.

King Henry VIII

Henry VIII was born more than 500 years ago. He was crowned king when he was eighteen years old.

◁ This picture was painted when Henry was old. When he was young he had fair skin and long red hair. He liked music, dancing and horse riding.

DATES	
1491	Henry VIII born
1509	Henry VIII becomes king
1547	Death of Henry VIII

△ Hampton Court was one of the palaces where Henry VIII lived with his family.

Henry had six wives. His first queen was called Catherine of Aragon. She had lots of babies. All her children died when they were very young except for one, a girl called Mary.

Henry wanted a son to become king when he died. So he decided to choose a new wife. Her name was Anne Boleyn. Before he could marry her Henry had to get permission from the Pope who was leader of the Roman Catholic Church. The Pope would not let Henry marry again. Henry was furious. He told people to obey him in future, not the Pope. Now there was nothing to stop him marrying Anne Boleyn.

◁ Catherine of Aragon.

▽ Anne Boleyn.

ANNA · BOLEYN · REGINA ANGLIÆ · 1534

Anne gave birth to a girl called Elizabeth. This did not please Henry. He wanted a son. He put Anne in the Tower of London and ordered that her head be chopped off.

Other people who Henry did not like were treated in the same way. He was now a cruel man. He took land away from the monks and nuns and shut down their abbeys.

Abbeys like this one in Wales became ruins. ▷

Henry spent lots of money raising armies and building ships. He went to war against France and against Scotland, but he never conquered either of these countries. By the time he died, Henry had used up all his money.

Henry's third wife, Jane, gave birth to a son called Edward. Henry was sad when Jane died soon afterwards. He married again but none of his other three wives had children. Many people were happy when he died.

Queen Elizabeth I

Elizabeth became queen in 1558 when her sister Mary I died. Elizabeth was very clever. Like her father, Henry VIII, she had a quick temper. A man who knew her well said: *'When she smiled it was like sunshine. Everyone tried to share it. But then came a storm and the thunder fell on all alike.'*

△ Great lords and ladies went with Elizabeth on her journeys to see the people.

England became famous for many things during her reign. William Shakespeare wrote great plays. Sailors like Francis Drake and Walter Raleigh explored new lands across the sea.

During Elizabeth's reign, people went to see Shakespeare's plays in theatres like this. ▷

DATES	
1533	Elizabeth I born
1558	Elizabeth I becomes queen
1603	Death of Elizabeth I

Elizabeth never married. This worried people in England. Who would become king or queen when she died? Some of them feared it would be her cousin, Mary, Queen of Scots, who was a Catholic. Mary was kept in a castle as a prisoner.

13

Mary's enemies said she was planning to kill the queen. She was put to death in 1587.

This angered many Catholic people, including King Philip of Spain. In 1588 he sent a large group of ships, called an armada, to fight the English. Sir Francis Drake and other brave seamen sailed out to stop them.

◁ This statue of Drake is in Plymouth, Devon. The English ships set out from here to attack the Armada.

Queen Elizabeth spoke to her soldiers to give them courage. *'I have the body of a weak and feeble woman,'* she said. *'But I have the heart and stomach of a king.'*

None of the Spanish ships landed. Some were damaged by the guns on the English warships. Many were blown by the wind on to rocks around the coast. The Armada was beaten.

△ The Spanish Armada is defeated.

The victory made Elizabeth very popular.
Most people were sad when she died.

This picture of
Elizabeth was painted
in 1588, after the
victory over the
Spanish Armada. ▷

King Charles I

As a child, Charles I was often ill. He grew up to be a small man and very shy. Pictures often show him on a horse. It made him look taller than he was. Charles thought he could do no wrong, because he believed that God had chosen him to be the king.

◁ Charles I.

When Charles became king he married a French princess called Henrietta Maria. She was a Catholic. People in England were worried about this. They thought Charles might become a Catholic too.

Men in Parliament were angry with the king when he tried to rule without their help. The row got so bad, the two sides went to war against each other in 1642. Parliament's soldiers were called Roundheads. Those who fought for the king were called Cavaliers. Sometimes a man on one side fought against his brother or an uncle on the other side.

DATES	
1600	Charles I born
1625	Charles I becomes king
1649	Death of Charles I

△ This is a scene from one of the battles in the war. In this battle the Roundheads defeated the Cavaliers.

Most of the fighting ended in 1645 after many people had been killed. The king had lost. He was caught and put on trial in a law court. He said his enemies had no right to do this.

◁ The trial of King Charles I.

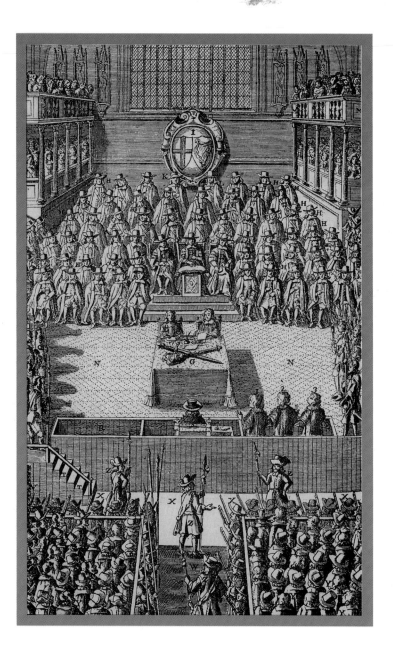

Charles was accused of betraying his country. The judges said he must die.

Charles says goodbye to his children for the last time. ▷

On a very cold day in January 1649 he was put to death. A man with an axe chopped off the king's head.

△ The execution of King Charles I.

People were shocked when they heard how the king had died. Some years later a black statue of Charles was put up in London. A new nursery rhyme was heard.

'As I was going by Charing Cross,
I saw a black man upon a black horse.
They told me it was King Charles the First.
Oh dear, my heart was ready to burst!'

Queen Victoria

Victoria was only 18 years old when she became queen. She wrote a letter to a friend. *'They want to treat me like a girl. But I will show them that I am Queen of England.'* In fact, she reigned longer than any other British king or queen. When she died at the age of 81, people were sad. Most were too young to have known another king or queen.

◁ Queen Victoria as a young woman.

DATES	
1819	Victoria born
1837	Victoria becomes queen
1901	Death of Victoria

Victoria married a handsome prince called Albert. He was her cousin and came from Germany. She and Prince Albert had nine children. The family was very popular. Buildings and streets were named after them.

△ Victoria and Albert with their eldest son.

Victoria was queen for 64 years. Great changes took place during this time. When Victoria became queen people who travelled a long way went in a stage coach. It took two or three days to travel from London to Scotland. When Queen Victoria died, the first cars had been invented.

At the start of Queen Victoria's reign, workers in Britain were famous for the goods they made. Prince Albert planned a big exhibition to show the goods to people from other countries.

◁ The Great Exhibition was held in a big building made of glass. It was called the Crystal Palace.

During her long reign, British soldiers conquered many lands abroad. Queen Victoria was very proud to rule these overseas lands. Cotton and tea were sent to Britain from India. Cocoa and gold came from Africa. Goods from these lands made some people very rich.

△ British soldiers sail up the River Nile in Africa in 1884.

Prince Albert died when he was only 42 years old. Queen Victoria was very upset. She wore black clothes for the rest of her life. In 1897 people from all over her empire celebrated her Diamond Jubilee. She had been queen for 60 years.

Queen Victoria as an old lady. ▷

Queen Elizabeth II

When Elizabeth II was born, no one thought that the young princess would one day be queen. Then, when she was 10 years old, her uncle, Edward VIII, gave up the throne and her father George VI became king. Elizabeth was older than her sister Margaret. This meant she would be the next queen.

◁ Princess Elizabeth at the age of 10, with her family. She is the girl who is standing. A few days after this photograph was taken, Elizabeth's father became king.

In 1939 a terrible war began. Elizabeth was 13 years old at the time. Planes dropped bombs on London. Some fell on Buckingham Palace. Millions of people died during the war.

Princess Elizabeth was in the women's army for a short time during the war. Here she is driving an army truck. ▷

The war ended in 1945. Two years later Elizabeth married Prince Philip. They had four children. Their eldest son Charles later became the Prince of Wales. He married Princess Diana. The other children were Princess Anne, Prince Andrew and Prince Edward.

DATES	
1926	Elizabeth II born
1952	Elizabeth II becomes queen
1977	Silver Jubilee

Elizabeth became queen in 1952. She was on a visit to Kenya in Africa. One day she was told that her father, George VI, had died. She flew back home as queen.

A year later, people from all over the world came to London to see her coronation. Many more people watched on television as the crown was put on her head.

△ The coronation of Queen Elizabeth II in 1953. Like most kings and queens, she was crowned in Westminster Abbey.

Since then, the Queen has been to many of the countries which were once part of the British Empire. People everywhere are pleased to see her. ▷

In 1977 Queen Elizabeth celebrated her Silver Jubilee. By then she had been queen for 25 years. Someone once asked her what she would have done if she had not been queen. *'I would have liked to have been a lady living in the country with lots of horses and dogs,'* she said.

The Royal Family. Can you name the people in this picture? ▽

Timeline

Year	King or queen	How long ago?
1050		950 years ago
1066	The Battle of Hastings **King William I**	
1100		900 years ago
1150		850 years ago
1200		800 years ago
1250		750 years ago
1300		700 years ago
1350		650 years ago
1400		600 years ago
1450		550 years ago
1500		500 years ago
	King Henry VIII	
1550		450 years ago
	Queen Elizabeth I	
1588	The Spanish Armada	
1600		400 years ago

The grey bars in this timeline show the length of each king or queen's reign.

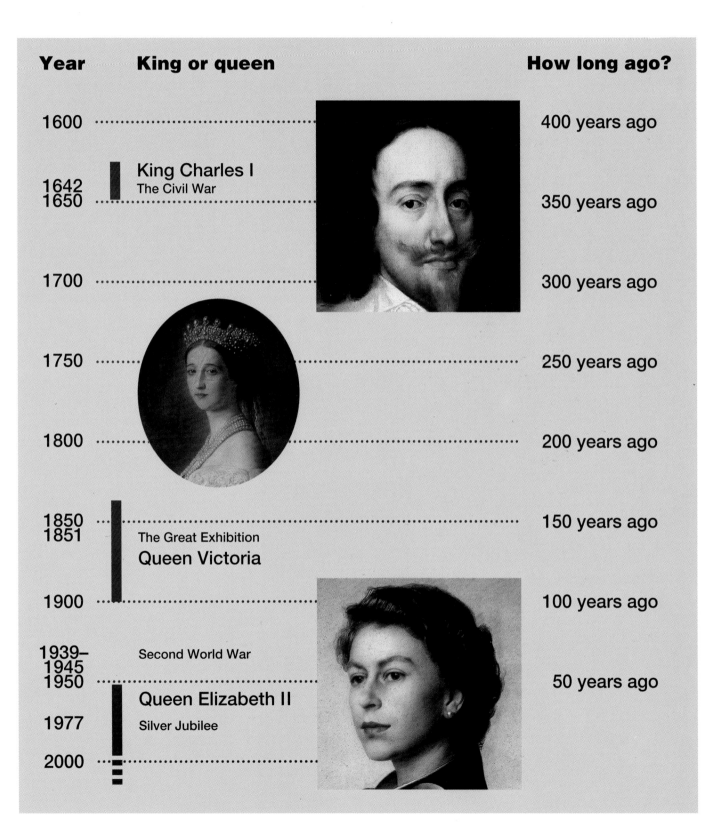

Year	King or queen	How long ago?
1600		400 years ago
1642 1650	King Charles I — The Civil War	350 years ago
1700		300 years ago
1750		250 years ago
1800		200 years ago
1850 1851	The Great Exhibition — Queen Victoria	150 years ago
1900		100 years ago
1939– 1945 1950	Second World War	50 years ago
1977	Queen Elizabeth II — Silver Jubilee	
2000		

Words to look up

abbey a building where monks or nuns live

armada a large number of warships sailing together

betraying being disloyal

British Empire those parts of the world which were once ruled by Britain

Cavalier a soldier who fought for King Charles I

conqueror someone who wins a victory over another country

coronation a service in a church when a crown is placed on the head of a king or queen

cousin a relative, such as the child of an uncle or aunt

crown a type of headdress with many jewels worn by a king or queen

Diamond Jubilee a celebration after 60 years

execution putting to death by law

exhibition a display seen by many people

monk a man who spends much of his life in prayer

nun a woman who spends much of her life in prayer

palace the large home of a king or queen

Parliament the place where people meet to say how the country should be ruled

Pope the head of the Roman Catholic Church

prince the son of a king or queen

princess the daughter of a king or queen

reign the length of time when someone is king or queen

Roman Catholic a type of Christian who believes the Pope is head of the Church

Roundhead a soldier who fought for Parliament

Silver Jubilee a celebration after 25 years

stage coach a coach pulled by horses, used for travelling long distances before the train or the car

tapestry a picture or pattern woven onto a piece of cloth

throne the place where a king or queen sits on great occasions

trial the judging of a prisoner in a court of law

Other books to look at

Great Battles and Sieges: The Battle of Hastings, by Philip Sauvain, Wayland, 1992

Look into the Past: The Normans, by Peter Chrisp, Wayland, 1994

Norman Invaders and Settlers, by Tony Triggs, Wayland, 1992

Tudors and Stuarts: Kings and Queens, by Tony Triggs, Wayland, 1993

Look into the Past: The Tudors and Stuarts, by Philip Sauvain, Wayland, 1995

Look into the Past: The Victorians, by Peter Hicks, Wayland, 1995

Some places to see

Battle in Sussex – where the Battle of Hastings was fought in 1066

Bayeux in France – where the Bayeux Tapestry can be seen

The **Tower of London** – where Anne Boleyn was put to death in 1536

Hampton Court, near London – the palace where Henry VIII lived

Westminster Abbey in London – where many kings and queens are buried, such as Elizabeth I

Trafalgar Square in London – where the statue of Charles I can be seen

Osborne House on the Isle of Wight – to see the palace which Victoria and Albert built

Balmoral Castle in Scotland – where Victoria and Albert spent many holidays

Windsor Castle in Berkshire – a favourite home of Queen Elizabeth II

Index